Baby Rodents

Bobbie Kalman
Crabtree Publishing Company
www.crabtreebooks.com

Created by Bobbie Kalman

For Otto and Olga Qundos
with lots of love from your Auntie Bobbie

Author and
Editor-in-Chief
Bobbie Kalman

Editors
Kathy Middleton
Crystal Sikkens

Photo research
Bobbie Kalman

Design
Bobbie Kalman
Katherine Berti
Samantha Crabtree
  (logo and front cover)

Print and production coordinator
Katherine Berti

Prepress technician
Katherine Berti

Illustrations
Barbara Bedell: pages 9, 10, 19, 24 (moving)
Jeannette McNaughton-Julich: pages 22, 24 (habitats)
Bonna Rouse: pages 5, 24 (lungs)

Photographs
Marc Crabtree: page 15 (top)
Photo Researchers: pages 19 (middle left)
All other images by Shutterstock

Library and Archives Canada Cataloguing in Publication

Kalman, Bobbie
    Baby rodents / Bobbie Kalman.

(It's fun to learn about baby animals)
Includes index.
Issued also in electronic formats.
ISBN 978-0-7787-1009-7 (bound).--ISBN 978-0-7787-1014-1 (pbk.)

    1. Rodents--Infancy--Juvenile literature. I. Title. II. Series:
It's fun to learn about baby animals

QL737.R6K325 2013   j599.3513'92   C2012-907325-3

Library of Congress Cataloging-in-Publication Data

CIP available at Library of Congress

Crabtree Publishing Company

www.crabtreebooks.com   1-800-387-7650

Printed in Hong Kong/012013/BK20121102

Published in Canada
Crabtree Publishing
616 Welland Ave.
St. Catharines, Ontario
L2M 5V6

Published in the United States
Crabtree Publishing
PMB 59051
350 Fifth Avenue, 59th Floor
New York, New York 10118

Published in the United Kingdom
Crabtree Publishing
Maritime House
Basin Road North, Hove
BN41 1WR

Published in Australia
Crabtree Publishing
3 Charles Street
Coburg North
VIC, 3058

What is in this book?

Rodents are mammals

Rodents are **mammals**. Mammals have hair or fur on their bodies. Most rodents, like this baby chinchilla, have fur coats. One kind of rodent has sharp needle-like **quills**, however. Which rodent is that? Did you guess porcupine?

baby chinchilla

*This mother and baby are North American porcupines. Babies are called **porcupettes**.*

Warm-blooded

Rodents are **warm-blooded**. The body temperature of warm-blooded animals stays about the same in both warm and cold places.

Breathing air

Like all mammals, rodents must breathe air to stay alive. Mammals have **lungs** for breathing air. Lungs are inside their bodies. They take in air and let out air.

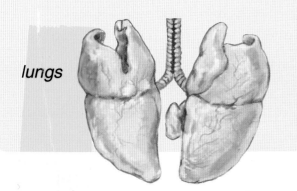

lungs

This baby squirrel is sitting in snow. It is warm-blooded, so its body temperature stays about the same in a hot or cold place.

These baby ground squirrels live in a hot desert. Their body temperatures stay the same, too. When they feel too hot, they go underground, where it is cooler.

Mothers and babies

Mammal babies are **born**. They come out live from their mothers' bodies. Many rodents are born blind and without hair or fur. Others can see and are covered in fur.

*Many rodents have **litters** of babies. A litter is a group of two or more babies born to a mother at the same time. How many babies are in this rat litter?*

This baby mouse was just born. It has no fur, its ears are closed, and it is blind. It will start to see in about two weeks.

Mother's milk

Mammal mothers feed their babies milk. The milk is made in their bodies. Drinking mother's milk is called **nursing**. Mammal babies nurse soon after they are born. As the babies grow, they nurse less often and start eating the same foods as the foods their parents eat.

This pet baby rat eats nuts, seeds, and fruit. It is no longer nursing.

These baby guinea pigs are nursing. They will nurse for three to four weeks.

7

Rodent bodies

Almost half of all mammals on Earth are rodents. Like all mammals, rodents have **backbones**. A backbone is a row of bones that runs down the middle of an animal's back. Animals that have backbones are called **vertebrates**. A rodent also has four legs, a head, and a tail. Rodents often stand on their back legs.

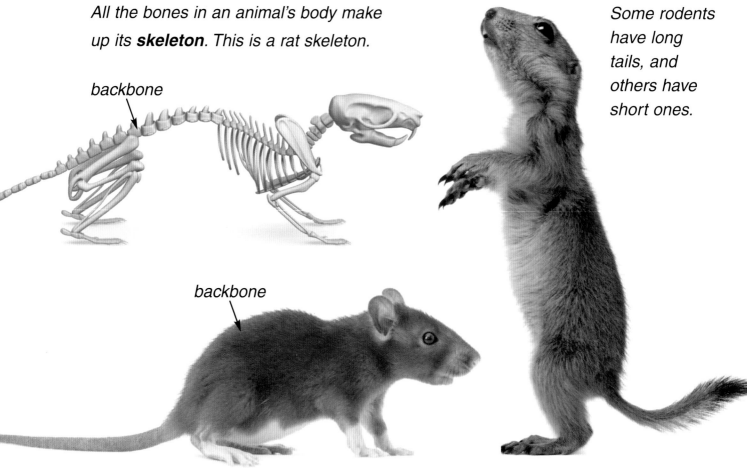

*All the bones in an animal's body make up its **skeleton**. This is a rat skeleton.*

backbone

Some rodents have long tails, and others have short ones.

backbone

Rodent teeth

A rodent has four sharp teeth at the front of its mouth. The teeth are called **incisors**. A rodent has two incisors on the top and two on the bottom. These teeth never stop growing, so rodents have to chew on wood or other hard objects to keep their teeth short and sharp.

Rodents have whiskers. Whiskers help them feel their way in the dark.

Most rodent bodies are covered in fur.

A rodent has toes with sharp **claws**, or nails.

upper incisors

lower incisors

Kinds of rodents

There are about 2,000 kinds of rodents. Some are tiny, and others are large. The largest rodent is the capybara, which lives in South America. Pages 10 to 15 show a few kinds of rodent families.

Pygmy jerboas live in Asia and are only about 2 inches (5 cm) long. They have long legs for hopping.

Adult capybaras grow to over four feet in length (120 cm) and weigh as much as 150 pounds (68 kg).

There are more than 1,000 kinds of mice and rats. These whistling rats live in Africa.

This tiny baby degu is related to the capybara. It lives in South America. Some degus are kept as pets.

Beavers are the largest rodents in North America. Beavers live on land and in water. They build homes in slow-moving water (see page 22).

The squirrel family

Squirrels that live in trees, ground squirrels, chipmunks, prairie dogs, marmots, and flying squirrels, shown on page 19, are all part of the big squirrel family. These two pages show some of these amazing rodents.

This baby fox squirrel is smelling a dragon fruit before eating it. Most squirrels eat mainly plants, but some eat insects and bird eggs, too.

ground
squirrel

chipmunk

Some ground squirrels have stripes. The stripes are only on their backs, not on their heads.

Chipmunks have stripes on their backs and heads. Baby chipmunks live on their own six weeks after they are born.

A marmot is a large kind of ground squirrel. This baby marmot is eating some grass. It lives on a mountain (see page 20).

Prairie dogs live in large groups. These prairie dog pups are coming out of their underground home (see page 22).

Porcupine babies

Baby porcupines are born with soft quills. Their eyes are shut for the first ten days of their lives. Porcupine babies nurse for several months but also start eating some plants after two weeks. After about six months, the babies live alone. They leave their mothers to find their own food.

This baby porcupine is nursing. It also eats plants.

This baby porcupine, snuggling up to its mother, was born with soft quills. Its quills will harden quickly like those of its mother's.

Baby pets

Hamsters, gerbils, mice, and rats are rodents that are often kept as pets. Rodent mothers look after their babies for the first three to five weeks. When the babies stop nursing, they are ready to be your pets.

Gerbil pups love to try new toys. They climb, jump, and dig.

Hamster pups are cute and fun to watch. They are small and do not need much space.

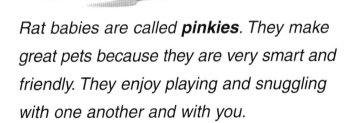

Guinea pigs are born with hair and are able to see and hear.

*Rat babies are called **pinkies**. They make great pets because they are very smart and friendly. They enjoy playing and snuggling with one another and with you.*

What do rodents eat?

Rodents eat different kinds of foods, but most are **herbivores**. Herbivores eat mainly plant foods such as nuts, seeds, fruit, flowers, grasses, and leaves.

This young squirrel is trying to eat the seeds in a bird feeder.

Porcupines eat all kinds of plant foods, such as leaves, twigs, and even tree bark. This baby porcupine likes eating flowers, too, like the one it is eating now.

16

What is an omnivore?

Omnivores are animals that eat both plants and other animals. Omnivores eat whatever foods they find so they will not go hungry.

Chipmunks are omnivores that eat fruits, nuts and seeds, and green plants. They also eat insects, spiders, small frogs, worms, and bird eggs.

bird eggs

insect

worm

Many mice and rats live near people and eat any food they can find. These mice are eating cheese, but it is not their favorite food. They prefer nuts, seeds, and other plant foods.

Rodents on the move

Baby chipmunks live mainly on the ground, but they can climb trees.

Rodents can walk, run, jump, and swim, and most can climb trees. Some rodents dig huge tunnels under the ground and climb up and down through the dirt. Some rodents can swim well and make their homes near water. One kind of rodent seems to "fly" from tree to tree, and another can hop like a kangaroo. Look at these rodents to see how they move. Name all the ways in which you can move.

Alpine chipmunks live on mountains and climb up and down the rocks.

Flying squirrels move from one tree to another by **gliding**, or sailing through the air. The flaps of skin between their legs act like a parachute.

Pet hamsters like to run.

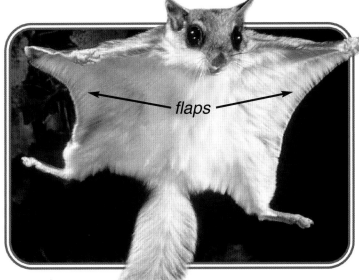

flaps

Pygmy jerboas use their long back legs for jumping the way kangaroos do.

(right) This baby capybara is swimming with its parents. Capybaras are excellent swimmers and can hold their breath underwater for up to five minutes. They can even sleep with just their noses above water.

Where do rodents live?

*This mother and baby marmot live high on a mountain. They make their home in **burrows**, or holes, under rocks. Marmots come above ground to find seeds, berries, and grasses to eat.*

Rodents live all over the world in different **habitats**, or natural places. Many rodents live in forests and grassy fields called **grasslands**. Some rodents live on high mountains, and some live in hot **deserts**. Deserts are dry places that get very little rain. Many rodents are pets that live with people.

Porcupines live in hot deserts, on rocky hills, and in trees. This baby porcupine and its mother live in a forest.

*Capybaras live in South America. Their habitats are forest areas near lakes, rivers, and **wetlands** like this one. Wetlands are lands that are flooded with water for most of the year.*

*These prairie dog pups live in grasslands called **prairies**. They dig huge underground homes (see page 22).*

This ground squirrel pup lives in a hot desert in Africa. It lives underground.

Rodent home builders

Most rodents live in holes underground or between rocks. Some live in trees. Some rodents, such as prairie dogs and beavers, build large homes that take a lot of work to make.

*Beaver families build homes called **lodges** in deep water. They use their sharp teeth to cut down trees and use the branches for building their homes.*

*Prairie dogs live in big family groups. Families dig large underground burrows, which are connected to the tunnels of other families. The burrows have rooms called **nurseries**, where babies sleep. The babies start going above ground to look for food when they are six weeks old.*

Are they rodents?

Some animals look or act like rodents, but they are not rodents. Do some research on the animals shown here. Which ones do you think belong to rodent families?

Hedgehogs have quills like porcupines. Are they rodents?

Big families of meerkats live in large tunnels underground that are like the homes of prairie dogs. Are meerkats rodents?

Rabbits have four long front teeth that keep growing. Are they rodents?

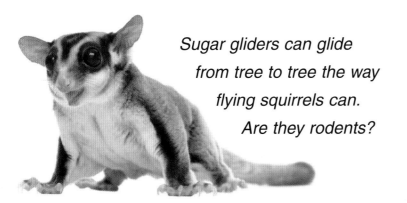

Sugar gliders can glide from tree to tree the way flying squirrels can. Are they rodents?

Answers

None of the animals shown here are rodents. Did you research what kinds of animals they are?

23

Words to know and Index

beavers pages 11, 22

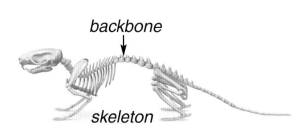

backbone

skeleton

bodies pages 4, 5, 6, 7, 8–9

capybaras pages 10, 11, 17, 19, 21

habitats (homes) pages 11, 13, 20–21, 22, 23

lungs (breathing) page 5

mice and rats pages 6, 7, 11, 15, 17

moving pages 18–19

nursing pages 7, 14, 15

porcupines pages 4, 14, 16, 20, 23

prairie dogs pages 12, 13, 21, 22, 23

squirrel family pages 5, 12–13, 16, 19, 21, 23